did yOu know?

There are over 1,000 known species of bats.
Most types of bats are small and could fit in the palm of your hand.

Have you ever heard anyone say someone is as blind as a bat? The truth is most bats have very good eyesight.

How many bugs can you eat? Yuck!!! One little brown bat can eat up to 1,200 mosquitoes in a single hour.

Many plants rely on bats for pollination and seed dispersal. Some of these fruits come from those plants: bananas, bread-fruit, mangoes, dates and figs.

Bill the Bat Baby Sits Bella

Illustrated by

Manuela Pentangelo

Written by

Daryl K. Cobb

10 To 2 Children's Books / Clinton

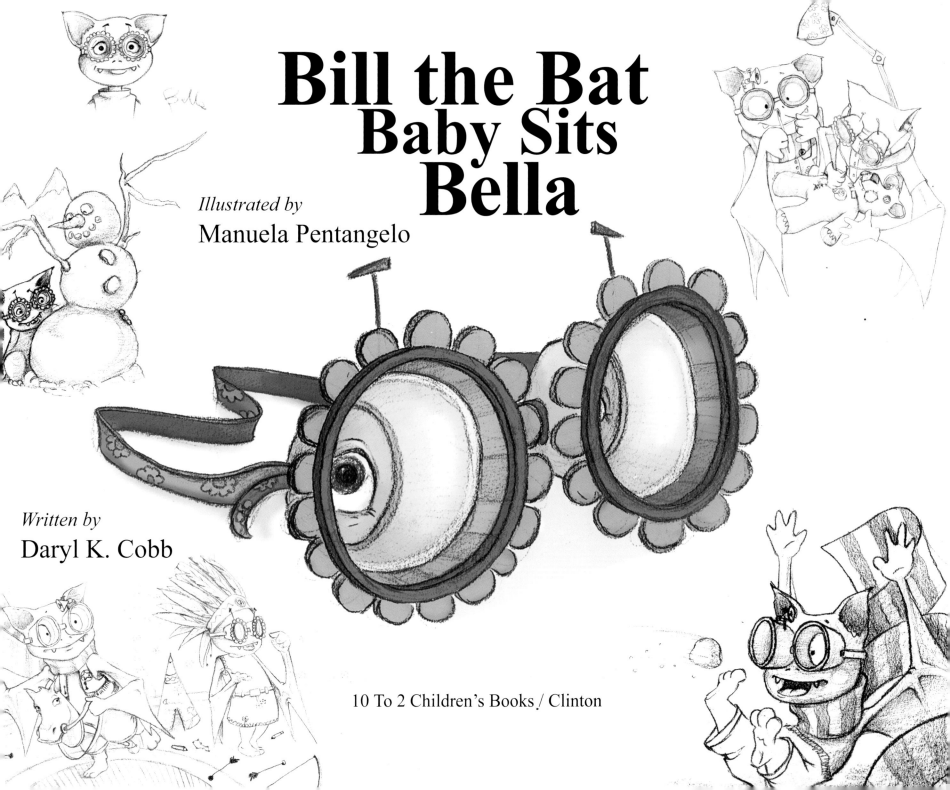

Library of Congress Control Number: 2008924579

ISBN 978-1-60585-818-0

Written by Daryl K. Cobb
Illustrated by Manuela Pentangelo

10 To 2 Children's Books

Time to Read

TM

Printed in China

First Printing 2008

I dedicate this book to families everywhere, for it is family that makes life special; and to my own family, who has provided years of memories and special moments.

Daryl K. Cobb

I dedicate this book to all my nephews and my brother.

Manuela Pentangelo

Bella, the youngest
of all the bat kids,
lived with her parents
and pet spider Sid.

Eight of the children
had all moved away.
"Went off to explore,"
her mother would say.

Her favorite, though,
was big brother Bill,
who didn't live far -
he moved down the hill.

He shared a house
on the outskirts of town
with a cat and a mouse,
near his friend
Hank the hound.

"Our trip
starts today;
Bill is coming,"
Mom said.

"I will clean up
his room and put
sheets on the bed.

Bella was busy
planning each day,
making a list of
the games they
would play.

On the porch of his house
Bill was saying good-bye.
"Bella's waiting," he said,
"I really must fly.

I hate to rush off,
but I can not stay.
I'll see you next week."
Then Bill flew away.

He flew by the owl
asleep in his tree.
Bill knew he'd be late,
it was well after three.

Bella saw him
as he flew up the hill.
She was tapping her foot,
unhappy with Bill.

"I have missed you so much!
I have missed you a lot!
For a moment there
I thought you forgot."

"Never," said Bill.
"I would never forget.
I have never, ever
forgotten you yet!

Not birthdays, Christmas
or sick with the flu.

Forgotten? Never!
Me forget you?"

Bella was smiling
from ear to ear.

She was so happy
her brother was here.

Their mom and dad said,
"It's time we must fly."
With a kiss and a hug
they all said good-bye.

"See you on Tuesday, sometime around four."
They leapt in the air and flew out the door.

Bella and Bill watched them both fly away.

"We'll call you tonight," they heard their mom say.

Bill and Bella
went right down her list.

Not one single game
on her list would
be missed.

They played every one,
some old and some new.

Some Bella made up.
Bill made some up too.

Bella made breakfast.

It's Bill's
turn for lunch.

They went to the zoo.
They took in a show.

At the top of the mountain,
they played in the snow.

Thursday,
Friday and
Saturday passed.

Sunday, Monday
and Tuesday
came fast.

"Bella,
we're home!"
said their mom at
the door.
"Not yet!"
said Bella,
"Bill, stay a
bit more?"

"I have to admit,
it has been quite
a thrill.
But it's time
to go,"
said big
brother Bill.

Bella was sad
when Bill said good-bye.
"Bella," said Bill,
"please do not cry."

Bill was surprised
even he was quite sad.
"Come see me,"
said Bill.
"Why not?"
said their dad.

"You're old enough.
    You know how to fly.
    You're a big girl now,"
    he said with a sigh.

She smiled as bright
as a warm sunny day.

"Bring your list," said Bill,
as he fluttered away.

Bill flew
out of sight
and did not
turn around.

His eyes
welled
with tears,
some fell to
the ground.

The frog, in the pond,
had been resting his head.

Something wet hit his arm,
"Is it raining?" he said.

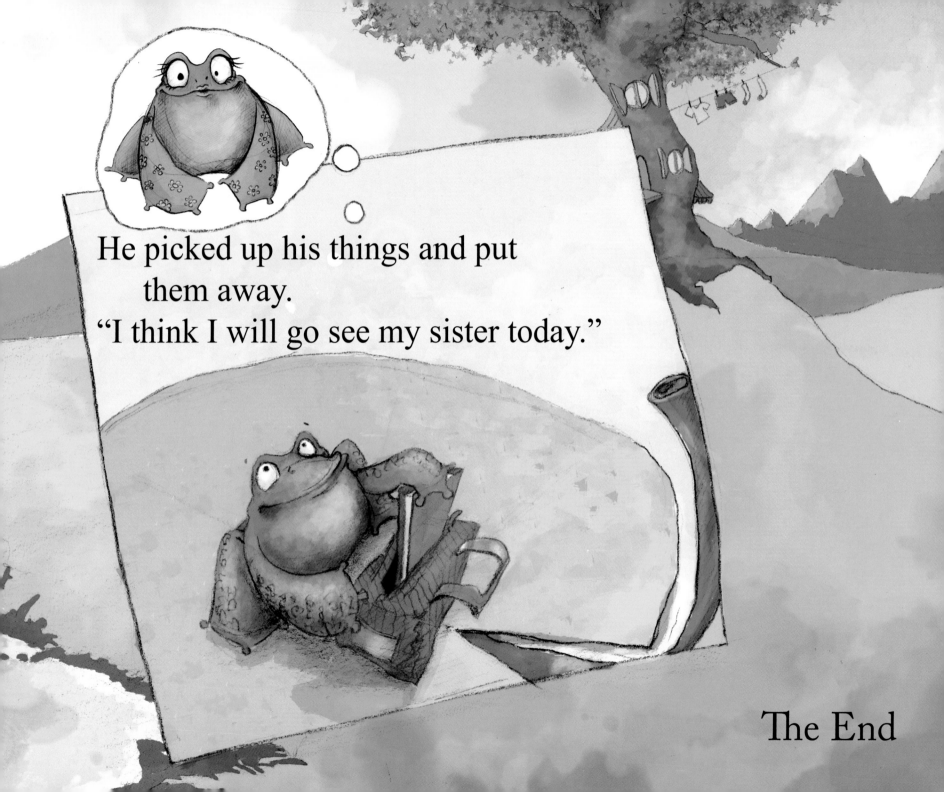

He picked up his things and put
    them away.
"I think I will go see my sister today."

The End

did yOu know?

A bat can detect tiny movements from great distances with its echolocation system.
This system operates off of sound waves and that is how bats find food in the dark.

Can you find a snack in the dark?

A single colony of 150 big brown bats can eat millions of rootworms, which would destroy a farmer's crops.

Bats rarely transmit diseases.

did you know?

The American bat species are in severe decline and some are already listed as endangered.

Without bats you will need a lot of bug spray!

Bats are very clean animals and groom themselves almost constantly.

Do you wash your hands before you eat?

Don't be afraid! Bats pose little threat to people and don't normally bite unless they are defending themselves.